Favourites

Anneli sundqvist

© 2023, Anneli Sundqvist
Förlag: BoD - Books on Demand, Stockholm, Sverige
Tryck: BoD - Books on Demand, Norderstedt, Tyskland
ISBN: 978-91-7785-576-7

Table of content:

My pray

I pray tonight
my life be light
no pain or cry... in sight
& I begging of more of joy... ashore
that's my pray tonight
goodnight

Tango

It takes two to tango

so, what do you say

shall we bite that red rose

and make that 'dance'

If your heart beat right

otherwise

of course

you can leave

you don't get that rose

between your teeth

Dice

Do you dare

to throw

your dice

In this game of life

will it be

something

good.

you

be a star

or a loser

just throw the dice

if you dare

you come the truth

a little bit

closer

Your 'you'

They say you are

false, untrue and unreliable

but I

love your 'you'

there below the surface

is the real 'you'

only I can, see?

a heart so nice

like yours

Heart of Gold

You

gold

diggers.

looking out for a heart

inside of someone

'soul'

if you find it

there is your gold

'a heart of gold'

Our sipping

Welcome to my world

no one here for now

but you and me

inside this cup of coffee

infront of us

hide the story just to be told

you and me listen

as you and me talking while we

sipping

because of that I love this cup of

coffee

Oh! What a cup can hide

welcome in and sipping

only for us

with our secrets close to heart

we talking tender

that's our sipping

Road

The road

is in front of you

I hope you make it through

it's a long road to go

will you make it through

lonesome road for one

but not for two

it

make life beautiful

if

you take my hand

so, I will walk

with you

Captain of the blue

Captain of the blue

wind in this world

play along with you

time to travel away

ship is in the water again

ready to go

somewhere just you know

Captain of the blue

time to go

so, again wind is in the sails

sead you away out to sea

to another time and place

life is wide

you travel around and try to

find

what you need

I hope

with a wish

you see me standing there

on the shore

waving good luck

for ever amore

you go go

but you are the captain of the blue

I put a tear down in the sea for

y.o.u

Secrets

Changes in life is nature of

life

You get to know while you go

the story of your heart

don't let it be untold

but keep some secrets close

to your heart

Just to share with your special

sweet heart

Two

Dinner for two

taste anything

on the menu I say to you

Fantastic food

but never more fantastic

then you

No: 1 in the menu

is you

Try to find my way

Street was rainy the light

had fade away

that night I walked the

streets after darkness

try to find my way

the wise man/woman say

look within

there you have something

maybe it telling you

something you need to hear

that little voice of wisdom

listen have an ear.

My friend

To live longer than you

my friend

it's a hell long time for me

to see me through

no one knows me more than you

my friend

what should I do

If, that day come like it do

for me or you

that will be true someday

but not for a while

let's hope that's true

The watch

Give and take

Wish

I wish

rhythm and style

in your talk

to me

to night

you steel my heart

every time

you talk tender to me

so, let me listening

to your sweet abc...

to night

Untold

A ghost in the night

and you are afraid of the

dark

So, you run, run away

from what's behind you

this is a night

with a ghost

afraid of the dark

so, you run

as fast as you can

let it be untold

Home

There is no end

of all the fun

days of joy

what we can do

it's true I

stay at home

with the light of love

in my home

'you'

Amor

The arrow of amor

is into my bleeding heart

Amor shot me

right in the spot of my heart

so, this arrow of love

is now right into my heart

With all this hurt

when love tortures the heart

with jealousy, anguish and pain...

what a hard day today

Amor with his arrow of love and passion

with all the pain, jealousy and torment within

that's from amors arrow today

what a pain

Bond

With your head on my heart

like a pillow

you rest your mind

in this beautiful moment

calmly you sleep

what a beautiful sight

a little new born child

on the chest of a mother

at this moment

love come to be the bond between the child

and the mother

Dr pill

Night time

sleepless night

tired no dreams

on the right path

in life

gonna be alright

if I just sleep a while

life is tomorrow's

Just take a pill you feel

alright they say

in modern life but who

believe

Dr pill is the painkiller

when it's a day

after night

In your veins

DRUGS IN YOUR VEINS

RUSHING FAST

THE SAME WITH

YOUR LIFE

RIGHT DOWN

INTO YOUR

GRAVE

Broken home

When you are a little child

Where do you belong

When everything is gone

Without mum, without dad

You feel you have no home

And you feel you on your own

Child of crisis, child of

Broken home

A homeless child

Where do you belong

A wise man said

"the path of the

Heart

Always leads to right

Destination

It leads you home to

Safe ground"

Child

My funny little child

so, young at heart

Live this life

as good as you can

put a little pray every day

say thanks for everything

you have

you are blessed believe in that

if you need some faith

you will pray for that

get to know the power of

yourself

inside your soul

make your day then rest in

the bed

dreamtime dream a little

dream

take a little nap

the night is there for you

relax my child

and remember I love you

until the end

of time.

Running wild

My imagination running

wild

what you do out there on

your own

without me on your own

I wait here for you

if you come back, I know you

true

I start to know you now

I think I believe in you

because I heard a 'knock' on

the door

yes, I believe in you

because that 'knock' was you

So alone

Love is lost

when I need it

the most

I don't make it

alone

need you

but you gone

so..alone

Meditate

If, your inner life

is out of life

you need one spark

to come a live

you can meditate

and find an answer

nou never thought about

so, meditate

you maybe find

what you asked about

in a way

you never thought

because life and meditation

is

something

that can make

changes of your mind

we never know

when, if, answers come around

in your thought

Stop 'ticking'

I count days, hours and seconds...

Nothing happens here at all at this moment

its quietly, only sound

is the clock 'ticking'

Years of my life running by

I spend my time this way, almost every day

sitting inside thinking about my life

I'm just a very old lady on the outside

but inside I'm thirty-five and want to

have some fun, and sometimes

I feel like two years old when I'm wearing a diaper

Soon I die right on the spot

boredom took my life

but it is not

stand in my obituary

because you all think I died from

old age

I want to have some fun

in this life so maybe, I forget the 'ticking'

I believe in human rights is to live a

good life

My old friends all lay down in the cold ground

I use to pray to the lord

to hold my hand, and when the day come

when its my time to go

I will meet them all, again.

when I'm climbing the stairs and

Knock' on heaven's door

my friend opens the door

that will be the day

my clock stop 'ticking'

(the day I stop counting days, hours and seconds...

and ticking')

Dream tonight

You are dead

still

we meet

We meet when I fall asleep

in my dreams

you still alive

so, I wish to dream tonight

I need it

to survive

..and I miss you, much

so, this is why

I wish to dream

this dream tonight

Further ahead

The road I walk

I know

it leads me forward

to

somewhere.

to a crossroad

further ahead

are you standing there

and waiting for me.

there

on the road

of

somewhere

this

thought

is like a light for me

to know... you standing there

and wait

for me.

faithfully.

Bravery

what is it

It can be many things in this life

we all need it sometimes

but if you do not know of it, for this day.

where will it be found

I think it is... inside.

Second chance

You and me we had love and

lost it

find love inside again if we can

we lost it once

twice we can find it

treasure from the heart

it can rebirth itself

Just look into the heart

be nice and kind to it

treat it well

the heart maybe answers

maybe it says 'Welcome' in

and start to love you

again

your second chance

Sip coffee

I'm here

with a coffee in my hand

Spending some time with you

and your coffee too

the best thing I can do

it's true

is to sip coffee and talk the

day through

with you

I've already left

Miss me... you do

even if I'm here in front of

you

so, you leave

because

I've already left

that's why you go. Away

that's why you don't stay

Don't

Don't say this

word goodbye

because I'm

not that strong

how will I

survive?

when to lose

you

is the worst

thing in life

River

If you don't love me

Just leave me

it's enough

without you I heal in time

day and night

but with you not loving me

I cry me a river

I drowning in

Snack's

Eat some snacks?!

let me taste

everything

with you

experience the beauty

of

sharing a moment

together

with you

(you and me)

Pray

I put out a little pray

to wash all sins away

I put the pray out to you

my friend

to put you on the right track

again

Family tree

Child

so little

but means so much

to mum and dad

and

the family tree.

the child is this little piece

of a loving family

and in this

big tree

they are

a bigger

growing family

Reality

Life is not a game

even if you win or lose

in reality.

every day of life

you live.

sometimes you wish

life was just a game

if you would die

you wish you still have life left to play

but...life is not a game

because

if you lose your life

you put yourself into your grave.

Happy people

When I fall asleep

I dream a dream

the dream was beautiful

but when I woke up

the dream was not real

why? It disappeared?

some people say

if you

live your dream you must

stay awake

they say

happy people

don't sleep

Little

Its

the

'little things'

that make

the

big

difference

Grave

Our days

those happy days

ended in a grave

today.

sad day

when

heaven took you away.

now

I must be strong

to carry on

happy memories of you

take me through

my heart is filled with

I love you

thank you

Soft

A naked skin

give thicker skin

with time

so, sensitive

to experience

life.

when life is hard

then you need

a soft heart

whatever you

going through

filter it

through your heart

Care

Give me

a smile

every day of our life.

I don't want your money

I don't want your car...

I just want you to

care about my heart

What price

I'm sorry I

never said

now I know

what price it had

you left me

I'm D.E.A.D

Timeless love

Holding that old dear

photography in my hand

looking at it day by day

when I looking at it like I do

then you looking back on me

smile and telling me

miss me when you gone

who can tell how old it is

timeless love

that's what it is

I'm looking for that spark

That little light

with life

that wake a dead alive

somewhere inside

it hides

magic of life

inspiration of life

'soul'

that electric light

Just talking

I'm collecting money

working down at the café'

serving coffee to everyone

take a sip, you feel just fine

talking to me down the café'

I'm a working honey

but I love my husband

I love him so dear

so, we just talking on this café'

Fare away

I know you are happy
but not with me
you out there without me
with someone else beside you
I standing here fare away
from the happiness inside you
I know I can be happy too
and I know I'm not for you
there is something and
someone else
for me, then
You'

If

If you not love me

you don't need to love me

Just leave me

it's enough

you don't need to tell me

were

you go

if you don't love me

I don't need to know.

Nature of life

Hope

please never fade in my mind

grow stronger every day

like the flowers that grow in

the ground

I do so too

I always try to survive

this is the

nature of life.

Now

Summer turned to cold

days be shorter as time go

faster than we know

the cold is all around us

where do we go from here?

nobody really knows what

time hides

we in time will know

take your watch and let go

life is 'now' there is nothing

else to

know.

Honey

I do
everything for you
honey
when
you cry
call on
Mommy
she be there
every time
you need
because
you in
her heart
always
through all the years
there is
no end
just a **forever**
in the
heart

Alone

Some days

I'm alone

but not lonely

peacefully I'm the only

my company with just me

is what I want this day to be

peacefully with me

alone not lonely

Morning light

I drink coffee in the morning light

my day start to show in front

of my eyes

I wake up

soon ready to go

after coffee now I'm ok

ready to make a move

and make my day

I'm ready to go, go go

Deep

Lost

in your eyes

diving deep

in

your beautiful eyes

so, sweet

My eyes

If I open my eyes

and look the world in another

view

what will I see

another picture

then before.

world change

infront of my eyes.

what I see

is just a piece

of my world

and another way

of life.

it all

depends on how I use my eyes

v.i.p

the history of

you and me

is written

deep in, in my heart

you are a lovely story

inside my heart

I use to tell pieces of this history

sometimes for someone I like

as it is like a part of my life

because

you are and will always be

a ..v.i.p

to me

in my life

A painting

A painting

there the paint has faded a little

nevertheless, it is nice

nicest thing

for me.

It is made by you

your joy

visible in the colours.

your brush strokes

as a story

there for me

to see

A whisper

It's a quietly whisper

from your own heart

a heart knows

so, you better be listening

on this quietly whisper

from the depth of your heart

The price

Life is a journey

we all pay a price

to keep us selves alive...

for this trip in life

is it wort the price

you must ask yourself

sometimes

Warrior

I deal with myself

every day.

In every war, battle I fight

in myself

there are no losers

The price

is experience

I won

in these battles.

Like a warrior

I am

I'm a fighter

The story

First, I was a little a baby

then a little girl

later a chick, a babe

a woman...

and a lady

and finally, an old woman.

after that you are dead.

that's how the story goes.

an interesting story

to be told.

Heart

You

v.a.n.i.s.h

into the dark

n.o.t.h.i.n.g left

but the n.i.g.h.t

in my heart

The mix

Mix

Of emotions

make your day.

it should be

boredom

all day

without

these emotions

you

feel in a day.

Mirror

Mirror reflects

a moment of truth

when I see into you

I see me

that's me

happy

to see you.

every day

we meet

this reflection

Of me

will I love myself

when I look into the mirror

tomorrow eve

Beautiful sight

Starlight in the sky
beautiful sight
a falling star...
wish of something fine, tonight
all I ever wish
is
everything going to be alright
for us

I wish love
inside of us
no fight
no war
Just love
for it all

my wish
is for us
tonight

Love song

It, something in a song
when
you must play it in repeat
memories it.
five years later
still love it.
it has melted into your heart
all this minutes, seconds and years you played it.
it yours, your own
from the first time...
and you still repeat it.

Today

It's like your smile is
magic,
trolls away this boredom day
this is the charm
of this day.
I enjoy your smile
you give today.

Reality

Heart beat

hard

in this reality

without it

it would be chaos

so, beat hard

my heart

Growing love

Memories of you
always be light
in my heart
growing love
when I think of you
you always in my heart

Artist

Let life be a palette

with all the colours

in the world

I be my own artist

in life

paint the world in the

colour of the day

power of the colour

make my day

tomorrow other

colours

then today

Love in it

Dinner

for two

talk out

what's in it

you can't cook

a dinner

If you don't

put love

in it

Communication

Hell of a day

when you come walking

through the door

Just remember 'honey'

always two side of a story to

be told

if we never listen on each other

how the story goes we never

come to Know

when communication shut

down

it ends with both go

Let it be me

Let it be me
to hear your thoughts in
your mind
tell me let me hear
everything nice
and bad things too from your life
I have a mind I have a heart
I respect if you not want to
share some parts
so, tell me now... let's start

Road of life

When we break

the love spells

what we awaken to

hell, or heaven or something

between them two

to survive

do something

with your life

which lead to good times

we must do what it takes

to survive

loving you

is what I want to do

but the spell is broken

so, there is nothing we can

do

but have faith

for the road of life

we walking

Best thing

I fight me through one more

day

but

without you

I would not do

I thinking

you

good to me

you the best thing I have in

life

I get by

'thanks' to you

Home

So lonely

on your own

if you want

remember my name

I be there right by your side

today, tomorrow every time

of the day

so, keep my number

your number is this number

the number to my phone

'home'

Fence

Jump over the fence?

grass is greener on the other

side?

or stay

I have everything you need

love is in my heart

so, don't jump

My love

You are on your own

fare away from me

the love inside of me to you

hold me through all these days

without you

my love

until the day I find you again

its people everywhere

but no one there like you

my love

someday you will be found

in the crowed of people

I find you again

love will live one more time

I know

you and me

is meant to be

someday

My love

You love so easily

in everyone you see love

you are blessed with love

that's why

I trust and don't trust in you

my love

Who are you

Never ever

I met someone

like you

who are you?

never saw you

before

even if

we always do

Sacrifice

Go with the flow

through all the days.

in your life

live every day.

make your sacrifice.

do what it takes to survive & stay alive

it's your life

we talking about

Death, in a tango

This time

death wants to dance tango with you

this passionate & dangerous tango

will it be the death for you.

I hope you have good dance feet

so, you can dance yourself out of this

when this day come

when

its your time to bite that black rose

and...

dance this passionate & dangerous dance

on

life and death.

If you don't make it out

It's your last dance

when the death, dancing with you

its like flipping a dime

crown is life, clave is death

If this is your finally dance you will find out

when you

take this passionate & dangerous dance

and bite that black rose

when you face

the death, in this dance of tango.

In a second

Love is there

for you

next second, it's gone

life can disappear

In a second

It can be

gone.

So, take care

of

all you got

life can change a lot

If you

be lonely

without

that special someone

that you

love

a lot

So, remember

Just in a second

all can be

lost

Regular people

Believe.

life...

what is it for you

believe in love & respect for

the living &

fight for human rights in

regular life

hope you do believe

alone is no good it can be

hard out there

on your own

we must become more so

Join

the army...solider

Sometimes life can be a

battle

do you have the courage

...strength

to take the fight

If not, I'm beside you

to put you on the right track

together we stronger than

the

lonely

dare to meet life

soldier

fight.

How about you

I have coffee cups for us

sit beside me and my little cat

we talk about everything

that 'pop' up in our heads

I love to talk yes, I do

so, I talk a lot to you

so, remember to listen

on what I say

I don't like to talk in repeat

I like the one that listen

You can talk after me

but

If I'm quiet maybe I'm sitting and thinking

so, give me some time so you notice if I'm listen

and when you speak

I promise to give you an ear

and I will take myself time to think

a while about everything that I hear

depends what you say and do

I answer you

when I'm ready to speak...

so, come and sit beside me

take a cup of coffee

with me

so interesting it will be

If you don't like coffee, you can drink the'

so, now we can dive into it

we leave the world outside

now it us and the coffee

let the time fly away.

when I start to speak

I forget if its Monday or Friday

and I loving it for real.

I'm more interested in you it

Isn't the coffee, how about you?

Its like I'm fishing in the sea

when you drinking, you're the'

if you interesting take a bite

and I catch a beautiful fish

for breakfast

you give me a little blink' with your eye

and I give you a little smile

that's feel alright

have you drink up your the'

do you want some more

this day is beautiful

I think it because of you

thank you

Enough

Are you the one

that stay

when my whole world fall

apart

or just when the world leave

will you be there

Just be... you and me

is that enough for you

Just be... with me

Favourite

Me

and my

honey

drinking

Coffee

always

gona

be my

favourite

cup of

Coffee

Trust life

I lost my life when you said

you leave

I'm all alone

I'm standing here you are gone

I'm all what's left of this life

what we had is gone

goodbye

Just to say hi! To start a

new life

if, I just try it be just fine

Its what I'm told from inside

'trust life'

Air

Love is in the air

breathe

It's just me

Sitting here waiting

for your call

that never be

and you sitting there as me

you know which way this will

take so don't do. This mistake

so, take the phone

and do this call

we both waiting for go, go go

Try

I try my best to live my life

without you

but I can't live a day

without to thinking of you

love finds its own way

I do know

give for a while peace in my

mind

my hope to get over you

so, I can live my life without

you

Is this hope...to not be weak

without you

Right thing

Stand tall

even if it blows

I know it's hard

that heart can break apart

but don't stop

keep doing your thing

In the end of the day

you can say

I did the right thing

Never leave

You
Tell me you need me
that you don't stay
if it's not for real.
I say, never leave

Blessing

Mistakes

everyone

do

sometime

If you lucky

Is goes well

everything be ok

again

forgiveness

is a blessing

if you need it, you

know

mistakes mixed with

love

is a good thing I know

sailor man

with the wind in its sails
the ship went out to sea
the woman wavering of goodbye
when the ship went away

the ship went back in again
but the woman was gone
married to someone else

the time had twisted the love
away
from this sailor man
free and lonely as he could be
at sea he went away
that's the life of this sailor man
to find love in another bay

Darkest day

Darkest day

when you broke your promises

and walked away

'our' time is now 'the end'

my mind and heart in a mess

and I must confess

my love was true

but it didn't mean much for you

you broke my heart

that's true

but I must understand

I must love

someone. Else

'now'

when it will be done

I finally be over you

So, I must be strong

and love again

and give a start for...

a 'happier' heart

Home

Out there

all alone

some people

make you feel

'on the way home'

Forever

So, many people in the world

but you are all I thinking of

you in my mind all of the time

I'm sitting on the moon

you are a star, you said goodbye

but not to my heart

love you for ever

you leave me for ever

punish and pain

sitting on the moon forever

you died but your name is

on my heart

f.o.r.e.v.e.r.

Worst

Find the word

that meant to be

that's worst

when you believe

it's me

All I keep

All I keep

Is

all the days we lived through

didn't remember what we do

only thing I remember

Is y.o.u.

I remember you and your lovely smile

that little one

that was my favourite one

so, I will remember you

from the first time we met

In my heart I love you I said

and I still do

do I miss you

yes

and I will always do

so, all I keep

are these lovely memories

Of y.o.u

Hid and seek

Cold wind of death will

'come'

One day.

With that last peace

For you

Or someone else.

That is the true rule

Everyone alive

In this life

No one of us

Can run away

Even if you try

Your best

To escape and stay alive.

In this way

you

someday

try to win some time

with

hide& seek

you hide

death seeks

but it won't do

because

wind of death

will simply find you

everywhere

whatever you do

the wind of death

will

take you away

of here

that's 'the end'

of you

peace over you.

But before that

Remember to

Live to your

Last breath

'stay alive'

Live this life.now

Child of love

You start the morning

with open your beautiful eyes

another day is just waiting

to be told like a fairytale

a day born by the morning sun

grow bigger every minute, second hour of the day

Its fun, so time sometimes

Just running away.

and finally find the rest in the sunset again.

I hope you make your day

because

with a blink' of an eye, its gone.

and in a moment its time again

to rest in the night again

good night

Child of love

I hope you made your day

something to remember

this is your childhoods days

keep it close to your heart

these days

because the day that went away

never come again

Friday again

Weekend days

has come to an end

now it's time to go back home

to my regular days

Monday morning. Just one more,

another day.

again and again, it repeats itself.

it put your mind in another way

but a working mind will find

rest

when it be

Friday... again.

Angels

I know the angels

I'm talked with them

so, many times

they use to listen

so, the luck is on my side

because of that

I can smile

most of the time

so, my life is light

even bright.

Beautiful heart

Your soft eyes

is like a nice shot

right into my heart.

you shot me

right deep down

in my heart

what a beautiful

shot

made by a woman/ man

with

a beautiful

heart

Sunlight

All days in the week

you take yourself through

I see

the sun light is in your eyes

and I see a little smile too

is it for me?

or people around you

tell me now

what will the answer be

that little smile you give

is it because of

me?

Wisely

When yesterday

passed away

you remember

the good

forgiving the bad

wisely

as you are

it's understood.

Darkness

Even when **darkness** only

thing on the road

you calm me down with your

words of love

Feel-good

I serve coffee

for you

if you want

me to.

take a sip

'feel-good'

is what I

want it to be

so, what do you say

is it ok... sugar, milk coffee

and me

But loving you

If I don't have you

I would not get through

the world would be too dark

for me to see with love

to get through Monday to

Sunday afternoon

and all over... again

that's true

what really worth to do

but loving you

Forgiveness

I don't know

but I believe

it's something there

for you and me

inside this beating heart

inside my mind

grow the feeling of a goodbye

for the old

this is the start to something

good.

a new start

forgiveness

is what I say to you

so, please take it to you

when I really mean it

my heart can't take you don't

forgive me too

when I mean it

Ground

Where ever

believe can be

for love, for the future or

anything...

it's the ground

for everything

Angel

Angel of mercy

hear me pray

I say my secret

take it away

give me peace

and mercy

Hard life

Loneliness

setting in

night fall

thinking of

you and me

I'm lonely as I

can be

you are dead

I'm the only

one here

and I know

'it's a hard life'

For me only

When you go

so, sad

I will miss the days

that we had.

so, I memories your love

for me

let these memories

keep the light for me

when darkness falls over me

I have our love in my heart

that don't leave me

lonely

this feelings & thoughts

for me

only

Love and care

For today

...I have a wish and prayer

filled with 'love and care'

for you

will it come thru

I hope it do

There are all kinds of people in the world

all of them need love and care

...one of them are 'you'

I hope you get what you need

every day

so, you have the strength

to face reality, every day.

I know

it can be a hard world

out there

when you are on your own

so, I hope life

treat you nice and kind

so, you keep the strength

to carry on

on your own

every day

in your life

This wish and prayer

are for 'you'

that need it

to face the truth

'that the world

can be so cold'

when you are out there

on your own

so, this love and care

is for 'you'. today

Guidance

In this dark

I'm in

I need to get some light

It is a daylight

I ask about

or is it a light

into my heart

I do not know, myself

maybe I need guidance

from you

it's

your inner light

I ask about

Difficult talk

When the night fall

and the sun goes down in the east

someone needs to talk to a priest

its hard time night time

for that someone

that need to make a call

and talk when crying

with the priest

Good intentions

Change track?

make your first step

that's good enough for me

good intentions

is the right track

The heart knows

An open heart

can forgive

what you do

because the heart knows

if you change

to something true

this is not the end

maybe a start... to something new

so, I forgive you

you blessed

if, you care stay that way

so, I don't need to give

forgiveness

again, and again...

Young at heart

You are young at heart

just a kid

in a world of people old &

young ones

Listen to their stories what

they tell

so, you grow up wisely

and to a good 'man'

find your place with the love of someone's

heart

listen well it's a good start

Red nose

The red nose

is in my pocket

just in case

throw it away

so, I do no

mistakes

throw it in

the dustbin

where it

belongs

Rest

I die inside more each day

to the ugly truth

you are gone

there is no me and you

on earth no more

I see up in the sky

sun shining in my eyes

the only light I have in my life

that thought burning me inside

what a life

I'm on page one what should I write

about my new 'life'

life without you

Lord, please help me through

I rest for a while soon is another night

moonlight in the dark blue sky

I fall asleep, dream about I met you

you said to me

'Some day we meet again, that

day will be a happy day'

so, I rest in these words

of love

Truly you

You and me

is it meant to be

or is your path

another heart

When I speak to you

you feel so true

in front of me

I see the real you?

is what I see and

what you say what I hear

really truly you

is this really you

if...I love this you

That heart

Make me a place in your heart

I don't want no other place to be

I like your spirit I like your soul

take me home to your heart

there I want to belong

don't leave me to stand alone

need you MUCH more

then before, I know who you are

you

the spirit with that heart

Me

Be me

is what I need to be

take the risk

you don't like me

this is me

I'm ready for?!

like me or not

One look

Love were you

felt it into

with one look at you

I knew

Set it right

If

you play your hand

that hand

that get you down

it's time to re-play

so, you set it right

time to know better now

and play your hand right this

time

put love and care in every

card, you have

or don't play out

your cards

you have on your hand

your heart makes your stand

for a happy day

let it be today you put it right.

Steal

The

time

is now

do you

steal?

sometimes

its ok

if you

steal

some time

with

me

Watch your steps

These hearts

filled with

love

and life

so

watch your

steps

so, you keep it

safe

New life

Don't hold on

to the things that hurt

inside.

leave things behind

get new ideas

do new things

get to know new people

and get a new life

that's the way in life

In your eyes

I want you to see

the real me

the fake...I can be...the best...I

can be...

in others eyes I'm maybe not

magically

but in your eyes

I'm the one. For you

perfectly

Loss & leaving

It takes a lot of rain

to understand

a heart can heal every time

its breaks

for me it not your heart

that beat for me anymore

loss and leaving

but life goes on

love is endlessly I know

now

because I find something

new

another heart

days of love and happiness

is here again

new life for me

love rebirth itself

'that's life'

Reflection of me

If, I look you in the eyes

what will I see

reflection of me

make you smile

or turn your head

another way

telling me

a nice and quiet

Goodbye

If

Write your

word in the sand

let it wash away

when tide

take it away

sometimes

let it all go

the nature

of life

If

unhappy love

If you be late

Love me or leave me

wish leave me don't mean

you don't love me

even if you not here in front

of me

because you just left me

I trust in you

when its knocks' on the door

it's you

happy to see you

every time you come back to

me

I believe you

If you don't come went

another way

love is over

so, if you be late... text me or

call me.

Love

You love thing

come closer its colder

when the night fall

fall into my arms

I hold you tight through the

night

outside the cold wind blow

its colder than yesterday

but you know I'm here to

keep you warm

we see us through we always

do

as long as I have you

Between the lines

When we speak
read between the lines
that's there the treasure
be found
you know what I'm talking
about.

My life

When the lights

goes out

in your eyes

I will miss your eyes

and my life

Monday morning

Love takes us through
even a Monday morning
so, if love is here for you
wake up don't miss it
because then you be without it

What you do with love
if you find it
treat it like a plant it grows
strong and wide
or forgot it it dies for you
you be without it
so be awake and take care
the chance is it be there
waiting for you
and say good morning to
you
taybe today

Today

Learned today

pain is strong

but love is

wide

it gives hope

for today,

tomorrows

even for yesterdays

Live love and laugh

I walking my path of life

night and day

I must be brave have trust all

of the time

Step by step I discover my life

I wish you by my side it gets

lonely sometimes

hold my hand

when I'm lonely and scared

share life when it's weird, funny or sad...

together we make this

journey not that bad

live, love and laugh

together with you

beautiful you, you changed my

life from bad and blue to beautiful

live, love and laugh

that what we do

Drive all day

Life can be

like a traffic light

with all these social rules in life

you know them you try to follow them

it just to understand them right

Red light: STOP, don't act at all

don't talk now, not at all.

pay attention all around

can be dangerous driving when

it's a red light on.

Yellow light: look up and wait a little while

because

it not time to go, yet.

rest and think a while

soon time to act and go

get yourself ready for...

175

the final one...

the happy green light: you can act now

so, just go.

you can talk now, so let's go.

everything ok

this is what you waiting for

All this traffic in my head

I drive all day until I lay my head on the pillow

in my bed

and dream away...

rest my mind of all this traffic in my mind

I made my day I'm ok

tomorrow its time

to

take a

drive, again.

Not for me

For real

life can be like a rollercoaster

if you handle it wrong

and I tell you it's no fun

to go upside down.

like a roller coaster ride

that it not how life should be

to live life with love and care that's how life should be

so, I say... no roller coaster ride

for me.

Better days

Hard time can knock' me down

so, I can't see the light of the day

I come through this misery

with the hope

tomorrows can be better days

to me

It nothing else to do but

believe it's true

its knocks' on the door

I see your face... oh! Better days

Your name

So many you

your name is

sweetheart, buddy friend...

every day they change

I love them all

because its

you

Nobody

Nobody really knows

what time is

when someone die

It the end of time

then you know

the value

of one second

one hour

three days

Worthy

The watch tick tock'

all of the time

I give it time

because I know

love is in my heart

I meet you again

sometime

then we talk

I think you

worthy of my time

of my heart

Everything

When you put your

smile on

you have everything

on

Secrets

What we

think

deep inside

are secrets

our alibi

is to not

talk out loud

Faithful heart

I'm the second thought

in your dreams I'm not even there

I been put outside the dream

when do you ever think of me

don't you see I'm the faithful

heart

don't you understand it in your

heart

right from the start you

were the one

bad odds to play along

so.

live without me

If you think of me

put a memory there

instead of 'me'

I'm long gone

nothing for you to see

faithful heart

left you on your own

you be

without me

you be on your own

so, think about it

if you not care

I'm

gone

Welcome

I can see

the light

of life

in your eyes

welcome back

to life

Easily

I love

so easily

I love a cookie...

as I love you...

love the weather...

love the moon...

sun is there too

as you see

love

can be

everywhere

even inside of you

The vision

in my head

say future is said

for me it's you

for all the days

It's true

my heart filled

with forever

y.o.u

If you lucky

Love is nice...to face

when life is cold...and the

cold wind blow

so, watch out

for that heart

if that heart beat for you

you blessed

it can see you through

if you lucky

it keeps its eye

on you

Hurt

You hurt me

deep inside

you don't give me

what I need

'love'

why are you so mean

Life call

I must accept the truth

love is gone

love not been here for long

love stone cold

it worse than hell

I been gone to long

good times gone

I need to

come back

on the right track

'life call'

Smile

Smile to fear

the fear disappears

Busy

When I ask you

about your life & plans

you tell me something

I can't give

you ask me about my life

but

I'm already busy

with

another life

.

Let's go

What to do

when things go wrong

don't you worry

experience make you grow

see things different

it is so

I learn from mistakes

I hope to get wiser for every day

every day a journey

so, let's go

Survive

Shadows fall stars above me

I will be ok I got you

hear your voice feel fine

feel love and tenderness

I know I will be ok

until the morning light

if days so ruff and unkind

it makes me feel that loneliness

but I survive

thoughts of you take me through

I will be ok I got you

I got you no one else will do

but you

you do what you do

that take me through

Surface

Fish in the water,

in the sea or in the ocean

free to swim and survive

these days it can be hard

days under the surface

Need

I'm in need

of kindness

show me you

that you have a heart

that I can believe in

I need it

can you show me

your beating heart

You

You

wear the key to my heart

you wear it so heavenly

key to my heart

is that smile and look

you giving me

Good to be

One step can make a difference

when even a little step

matters

It takes you forward

so, please step one step

as you feel

if good intentions

then its really good to be

Roulette

Roulette

like a

gun to your head

playing high

with your life

love without a head

is

roulette

No regrets

When you

live your life

scared to look life

in the eye?

sometimes

but if you do.

remember look with love

you live

this life

with

no regrets

Menu

Check in the menu

if it's something new

in the menu

in front of you

you see me

sitting there

will I do

am I on the menu

for you

Mystery

Mystery of your thoughts

tell me

a line

about your life

something changes

I understand

Timeless date

Summer turned to cold.

when Octobers face came in

I remember the summer days

my summer love with you

I save it in the depth of my heart

memories of

me and you

'a timeless love'

that what it is

it takes me through this cold October days

and the winter land

the memories of the summer

with a timeless date

Stay

Love

is real

when you

are there

for me

you always around

in my mind

memories of you

all your heart

make that stay

into my mind

you will rest in my heart

one day

Somethings wrong

I don't like you

is that wrong

because you bad

doing me wrong

you the bad one

I'm the sad one

somethings wrong

Upon your eyes

I built my dreams upon

your eyes

every time I look into them

my dream come through

my dream is you

all I want to do

is to...

breathe you in

and live a little

You

Once upon a time

I felt happiness inside

as years went by

one by one

what made me happy

it was you

you were there

right by my side

my memories of you

I keep them deep inside

now when you are gone

and our days are done

memories of

you stay

safe here

right

down

in this heart

Of mine

Snow snow snow

When I woke up this

morning

It was snow outside my door

The sun was gone

and the snow just fall and fall

Summertime gone a long time

ago

and now the autumn is gone

too

that's for sure

nature is white its winter land

outside

my door

when I step outside, I slip

and fall

and its cold for my toes

so, I thinking of stay at home

in my warm house that is my

own

happy inside when the cold

wind blow

little song about winter all

day long

I create in this time of year...

and month

This way I killing time in a

fun way

so let it snow, snow snow...

Heal me

Let your heart beat

then I know

its good times here

I want to hear

that beat today

heal me

I believe I need it

today

Fool

When I think of you and me

I wondering

what you see in your heart

when you see or think of me

does I count

or am I just another fool

Dream

I wish you miss me in your

life

That I am the one you dream

about

maybe you dream like me

but the dream not come

through

its nobody there but the air

what happened with my

dream of you?

you ask yourself and feeling

blue

But if you open your eyes

and see

dream can be real if you

just try

your dream can be here

with... me

Questions inside

Questions inside

they wake every time

I see you

am I cool for you, just a fool...

or do you see me true

I wish I could read your

mind

I wish I knew

to ask would be too much

you see

it means so much to me

what you think, feel and

what's on your mind

Oh! This questions inside

they wake every time

I see you

or think of you

all of the time

Angel

Someday my life is over

I fly away be that angel

you

love from above

I sending you love

everyday

because I love you

in every way

The moon

On this planet earth

so many people

but me only so lonely

its like I'm sitting on the

moon

dreaming my life through

where ever I look there are no

you

Just me... on this planet earth

but it feels like the moon

since you left me

I feel this way... I do

Busy

Shoes on the hall floor

all in a mess

people don't see the mess

busy living a life

so, this mess

just out of sight